Li'l Woodzeez® is a Registered Trademark of
Maison Battat Inc.
Text Copyright © 2017 by Susan Hughes.
Edited by Joanne Burke Casey.
All rights reserved, including the right of reproduction
in whole or in part in any form.
ISBN: 978-0-9843722-1-8
Printed in China.

Welcome to Honeysuckle Hollow®

where all the woodland creatures work together
to take care of each other and their environment.

Every animal family has a special job and every day is an
adventure. With their creativity, generosity and sweet
spirit, these friends make chores chockfull of fun.

Meet more Li'l Woodzeez® families
in the back of this book.

Wally and Dixie Whiskerelli purred happily. They liked putting the toppings on pizzas for their family's food truck.

It's called "Honeysuckle Sweets & Treats."

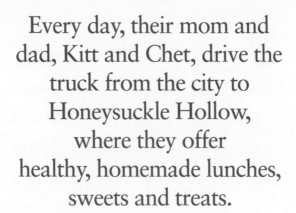

Every day, their mom and dad, Kitt and Chet, drive the truck from the city to Honeysuckle Hollow, where they offer healthy, homemade lunches, sweets and treats.

And every day, there is a surprise Special of the Day!

Kitt can make something tasty
out of any ingredient.

Customers often bring her
different ingredients just
to see what she'll create.

Earlier, Stripe Diggadilly
had dropped off a basket
of zucchini.

"What will Mom's Special
of the Day be today?"
Wally asked his dad.

Chet shrugged, but he
had a twinkle in his eye.

"I don't know,
but we'll soon
find out!" he said.

Chet was right.

That afternoon, the Whiskerellis' woodland friends lined up for Kitt's Special of the Day.

"This zucchini bread is melt-in-your-mouth good!" they said.

The next day, Kitt did
it again.
She transformed
a wheelbarrow-load
of peas into
scrumptious pea soup.

Another day,
Kitt turned
a bucketful of sweet
potatoes into
fantabulous
sweet potato fries.

The day after that,
a basketful of
pumpkins became
out-of-this-world
pumpkin pies.

But then, Star Hoppingood
arrived with a big sack.

Wally and Dixie
peeked inside.

"Turnips! Not even Mom
can make cooked turnips
taste good!"

Word spread. That afternoon, everyone arrived early.

"What meal will 'turn up' today?" joked Pete Whooswhoo.

The other customers were too worried to joke. Not one of them liked cooked turnip!

Would Kitt's Special of the Day be the Flop of the Day?

Suddenly Kitt appeared,
with a grin on her face.

"Welcome, all! Today's
Special of the Day is...
Terrific Turnip Salad!"

"This salad has lots
of yummy
chopped vegetables,"
Kitt explained.
"And it's topped with
shredded raw turnip."

Raw turnip, not cooked.
No one had ever thought
to try it *raw*.

Everyone's eyes lit up.
And everyone
ordered the salad.

"Kitt's Terrific
Turnip Salad really
is terrific!"
everyone cheered.
"Kitt did it again!"

Yes, it was the
most popular
Special of the Day yet!

The Snipadoodles™
Sheep Family
*Baabaa Spa
& Hair Salon*

The Scamperscoot™
Chipmunk Family
*Scoops & Sprinkles
Ice Cream Shop*

The Skyhopper™
Panda Family
*Sunny Skies
Airport*

The Canberra™
Koala Family
*Toowoomba
Acting Troupe*

The Tippytail™
Fox Family
*Cares-a-Lot
Kindergarten*

DZEEZ® FRIENDS & BOOKS

The Woofwinkle™
Dog Family
*Li'l Luvs & Hugs
Nursery*

The Whiskerelli™
Cat Family
*Honeysuckle
Sweets & Treats*

The Healthnuggle™
Bear Family
*Healing Paws
Health Center*

The Tidyshine™
Turtle Family
*Clean-as-a-Whistle
Tidying Service*

The Whooswhoo™
Owl Family
*Nighty-Night-Sleep-Tight
Safety Service*

COLLECT ALL!

The Bushytail™
Squirrel Family
*Tickle-Your-Taste-
Buds Bakers*

The Hoppingood™
Rabbit Family
*Hoppin' Healthy
Harvesters*

The Diggadilly™
Raccoon Family
*Reduce, Reuse &
Recycle Crew*

The Waterwaggle™
Beaver Family
*Busy Beaver
Launderette*

The Swiftysweeper™
Hedgehog Family
*Sweep, Mop, Sparkle
& Shine Specialists*